This book celebrates the everyday actions taken by Taulians and their families to make a positive impact.

Through these stories, we hope you'll be inspired to discover small yet meaningful ways to contribute to a sustainable future.

Together, every effort, no matter how small, truly counts.

Use Less Energy

Turn off the lights when you leave a room

"We turn off the lights when we leave a room to conserve energy."

The Saia-Marchese Family

Recycle

Separate paper, plastic, and glass into different bins

"Our family makes an effort to recycle to save the planet."

The Halden Family

Upcycle

Create crafts from old items

"We love turning household waste and recycling into beautiful works of art!"

The Glotfelty Family

Grow a Garden

Plant your own veggies and flowers

"It makes us happy to plant a seed and watch it grow into food we can eat."

The Douglas Family

Save Water

Turn off the water while brushing your teeth

"To save water, we never leave the tap running
while we brush our teeth."

Gurnaz Sharma

Inclusive Play

Make sure playground games include everyone

"We promote an inclusive mindset by playing with diverse dolls in all ages, races, sizes and hair colors."

Lara Sear & her Doll Squad

Homemade Gifts

Make your own gifts at home to save materials

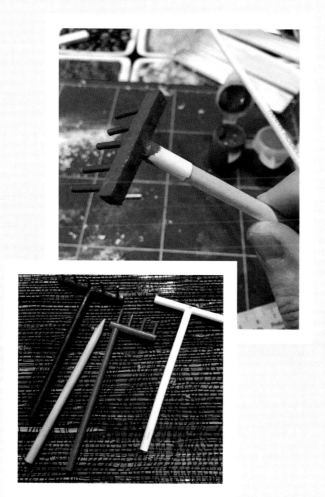

"I love making gifts, especially when they involve DIY. For one of my favourite projects, I crafted a set of tools for a friend's zen garden using wooden sticks, an old wire coat hanger, toothpicks, glue, acrylic paint and nail polish."

Pavel Ivanov

Clean Up Litter

Pick up trash in your neighborhood or park

"When we go on walks, we carry a bag to pick up litter, keeping our neighborhood clean and green."

Molly McConnell & Clover

Share Toys & Books

Share with friends to reduce waste

"Toula likes to rescue unwanted toys found on walks, quickly transforming them from trash to wag-worthy fun!"

Toula Staub

Learn About Animals

Discover why animals need clean places to live

"We care for our local outdoor cats by providing them with shelter, food, and water."

The Brown Family

Use Public Transportation

Ride the bus or train to reduce air pollution

"We take public transit and walk as much as we can in Montreal - specially in the Montreal metro."

Léo & Aurélie Nicolau

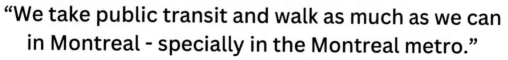

Turn Off Electronics

Unplug devices when not in use

"In order to save on electricity, I unplug smaller devices and turn off bigger devices when I am done using them."

Rebeca Brown

Buy Second Hand

Shop for clothes and toys at thrift stores

"We love treasure hunting at local thrift stores!"

The Elvira Family

Support Wildlife

Create bird feeders or plant flowers for bees

"We care about wildlife and biodiversity. We built bug and bird shelters to protect them from bigger predators."

Arthur & Adrian Sing

Donate Clothes and Toys

Give away items you no longer use to those in need

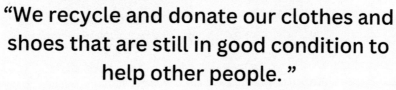

"We recycle and donate our clothes and shoes that are still in good condition to help other people. "

The Hopkinson Boys

Plant a Tree

Trees clean the air and provide homes for animals

"We gather and plant acorns and pine cones, nurturing them until they're strong enough to return to the forest."

Daniela's Family

Rescue an Animal

Save a pet from the shelter and help make space for another animal in need

"We got our dog Tilly from Safe Hands Rescue."

"Kitty Lacey we found by a boat landing and cat Gary outside in the pouring rain."

The Krebsbach Family

Help Neighbors

Offer to help neighbors with chores or errands

"We regularly run errands for our neighbors. It feels good to show support through acts of kindness."

The Schein-Butynes Family

Gratitude Journal

Each day, write down things you are thankful for

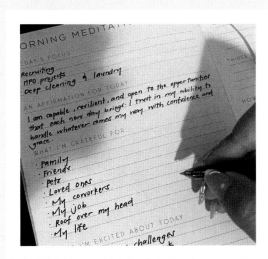

"Writing in my gratitude journal helps me focus on the positives in my life, shift my perspective, and find joy in the little things."

Lugill Carreon

Talk About Your Feelings

Share how you feel with someone you trust

"In our house we know it's important to talk about our feelings because they help us understand ourselves and each other."

Talia & Penny Velazquez

Nature Walks

Get outside and enjoy nature to feel happier and have fun

"We went on a family vacation that spanned 4,000 miles and took us to new heights and incredible adventures."

The Trost Family

Take a Break

Take time to rest and relax during a busy day

"We love heading out-
doors to take a break
after a long day.
Especially with our
Mickey Mouse ears on! "

The Tumrukota Family

Explore Hobbies

Try new and fun activities to find what you love to do

"After school, I like to make cakes, cookies, and ice cream to feed my curiosity and food tastes."

Aurelius Boehme

Compost

Turn food scraps into garden food

"We use a countertop composter to turn our food scraps into soil for our little veggie garden."

The Hughes Family

Educational Shows

Watch shows that teach you about the world

"We always find a historical period to be passionate about, and watch all the documentaries about it."

The Nikolovi Family

Water Plants with Rainwater

Collect rainwater for your garden

"We collect rain water in a barrel connected to our gutters, which we then use to water our plants and garden."

The DeBate Family

Read Books

Read lots of books to learn new things

"We read books to cut down on screen time. This helps us connect as a family."

Janelle Swanson & Robin Lazaro-Swanson

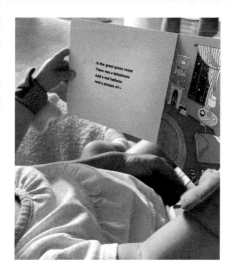

Create Art

Draw, paint, or make crafts to express your feelings

"Drawing helps us express our thoughts, triggers our creative minds, and improves our engagement with our siblings."

Tashlyn, Princeton,
Rachelle & Sheralyn Su

Exercise and Play

Stay active to keep both your mind and body healthy

"I exercise everyday by myself, with my bunnies, or with my family. I stay active to keep my body and mind healthy."

Lucy & Zoe Mienie

Reusable Bags

Use cloth bags instead of plastic ones

"I always carry a reusable cloth bag for spontaneous purchases to reduce waste and protect the environment."

Samantha Blai

Volunteer

Participate in community services with your family

"Our family has volunteered at community events like recycling drives and the animal shelter, where my children always wanted to bring home all the kittens."

The McIntyre Family

My Sustainability Checklist

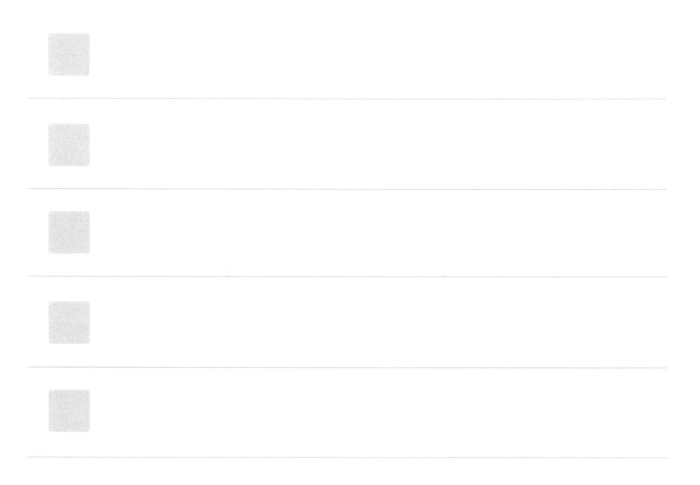

Photos of Me in Action

Add more photos here

...and here!

Don't be shy. Add some photos.

Don't forget this page.

...and this page.

It's your book,
add some photos.

A special thank you to Rene Ho for generously funding the printing of this book, allowing us to share it with everyone who participated.

We also want to thank Darcy Douglas, Danny DeBate, and Jade Sear for all their incredible work, from designing the book to preparing it for print, making it something Taulians can share with their family and friends.

And thank you to all the Taulians who contributed their stories and actions — this book wouldn't exist without you.

Made in the USA
Middletown, DE
09 December 2024

66426282R10042